The Puppy Collection

# Cricket's Close Call

## Susan Hughes

Illustrated by
Leanne Franson

SCHOLASTIC INC.

Thank you to Dr. Stephanie Avery, DVM, for her puppy expertise.

First published in Canada in 2015 by Scholastic Canada Ltd.

ISBN 978-1-338-16060-4

12 11 10 9 8 7 6 5 4 3 2 1                                        17 18 19 20 21 22

Printed in the U.S.A.                                        40

This edition first printing, January 2017

*To Ella Dembo and her dogs,
little Maia and large Enzo*

# CHAPTER ONE

*The puppies were taking over the classroom! A black and white border collie puppy stood on Ms. Mitchell's desk. A fluffy white Samoyed puppy with a curly tail peeked out of the garbage can. Four greyhound puppies tumbled together on the carpet at the front of the class.*

Kat sat at her desk with her pencil in her hand. She had finished her math problems. Now she was having her favorite puppy daydream.

Her eyes were open, but all she could see were puppies.

Ms. Mitchell smiled at Kat. "You have a tough decision to make," she told Kat. "Which puppy are you going to choose?"

"I can have one?" Kat asked, surprised.

"Of course you can," said Ms. Mitchell. "Your parents said so."

Kat grinned. But which one would she choose? Maybe that cute bulldog puppy with the wrinkly face, pouncing on the chalk brush. Or the playful Labrador retriever pup wrestling with the poodle. Or maybe . . .

The bell rang.

"Let's go!" said her friend Grace. But how could she choose? The Great Dane pup was adorable. The pug was so sweet! The collie was . . .

"Kat, let's go!" said Grace again. She sat at the desk right next to Kat. "The bell rang. School's over."

Kat blinked and returned to reality. In today's daydream, her teacher had said she could have a dog. She had said it was okay with Kat's parents. But Kat knew she wasn't really allowed to get a dog. Her parents still said they were too busy to look after a puppy, even though Kat said she would do all the work.

"Kat," Grace said. She gave Kat a nudge. "You said we had to hurry to Tails Up after school today. Remember?"

Kat grinned. "Of course!" she said. "Let's go!" Maybe she couldn't have her own puppy, but she had something almost as good! She had an aunt who owned a busy dog-grooming salon, Tails Up! Grooming and Boarding.

As Kat and Grace hurried to the door of the classroom, Ms. Mitchell called, "Off to Tails Up, girls?"

Kat smiled. "Yes, Ms. Mitchell."

"So your aunt's business is doing well," Kat's teacher said. "I'm glad!"

"Aunt Jenn hired an assistant to help answer the phone and book appointments," Kat explained. "His name is Tony. But even so, Aunt Jenn is very busy. So she needs Grace and Maya and me to help out with any puppies that are boarding there."

Grace had lived on a farm right up until that autumn. Then her family moved to the town of Orchard Valley.

Today, like most days, she wore her long red hair in braids. *Just like Anne of Green Gables*, Kat thought.

"We're just meeting up with Maya now," Kat added.

Maya was Kat's best friend. The two girls had been best friends forever. They had known each other since nursery school. Until this year, they had always been in the same class. But this year Maya was in the grade three-four split class, and Kat was in the grade four-five split class. Kat had made friends with Grace, who was new in her class. And now Grace and Maya were friends, too.

Kat and Maya were still getting to know Grace. She was quiet. She had trouble saying how she felt about things. But all three of them had one important thing in common. All three of them loved dogs.

"Well, have a wonderful time," said Ms. Mitchell, her eyes sparkling.

Kat and Grace hurried out of the school. Kat spotted Maya waiting under the oak tree at the school gate.

"Here come the slowpokes," Maya said, as the girls drew near. She put her hands on her hips and pretended to yawn. "I have been waiting for-*ever* and a day."

"Sorry," Grace said. "We didn't mean to be late."

But Kat just grinned. She knew not to take Maya's teasing too seriously.

"I will forgive you," said Maya, with a royal wave of her hand and a wink at Kat, "but only if you tell me the answer." She raised her eyebrows at Grace.

Grace frowned. She shot a worried look at Kat, then looked back at Maya.

"The answer!" said Maya. "The answer to Katnip's joke!"

Every day Kat told a joke to her friends. Some days she told it before school and made Grace and Maya wait until the end of the school day before she would tell them the answer. This morning, the joke was "How do you keep a dog from barking in your front yard?"

"Right!" Grace grinned at Maya. "But are you sure we really want to hear it? It'll probably be a groaner."

"Good point," agreed Maya. "But you know, I just can't stand the suspense. I have to know. Kat? Spill."

"Okay. You asked for it." Kat shrugged. "How do you keep a dog from barking in your front yard?" She paused. "You put him in your backyard."

"Agh!" moaned Maya and Grace.

"Worst all-time joke," Maya announced happily, as they all hurried toward Tails Up.

# CHAPTER TWO

The bell jingled as Kat, Maya and Grace opened the door to Aunt Jenn's salon.

"Hello, ladies!" Tony waved at the girls from behind the front desk. He was the new office helper. "Your aunt will be out in a moment," he told Kat.

Marmalade, Tony's fifteen-year-old tabby cat, sat on the countertop. Tony said that Marmalade wouldn't let him go anywhere without her.

"Hello, Marmalade," said Grace. She went right over and stroked the cat. Like always, Marmalade pretended not to care. "Oh, I know," said Grace. "You don't like people at all, do you?" Marmalade refused to look at the girl. But she couldn't stop herself from purring contentedly.

As usual, the waiting room was crowded. A young girl in jeans and a T-shirt was practicing "shake a paw" with her bearded collie. A white standard poodle sat at the feet of a woman who wore her hair in a bun, an elegant skirt and jacket and a string of white pearls. Dainty glasses were perched on the woman's nose.

Two large men were sitting side by side on the couch. Each wore a black leather jacket and pants with silver studs and black boots. One man was bald. One had a mustache. Each had a motorcycle helmet on his lap. *They look tough*, thought Kat.

"German shepherd," said Maya. She added, "Or

Doberman pinscher." It was one of their favorite games. When she and Kat saw a person, they named the dog breed he or she most resembled. Sometimes it turned out to be the breed of dog that person owned.

Kat nodded. That made sense. Tough dogs for tough guys.

The door to the grooming room opened. Out came Aunt Jenn wearing her baby blue grooming coat. Her hair was pulled back in a messy ponytail. In her arms were two black pugs. Each was wearing a black collar with silver studs.

The biker dudes stood up, and Kat and Maya turned to each other with their eyes wide. They slapped their hands to their mouths to keep from laughing out loud.

"Here we are. Zack is for you, and Zeke is for you," said Aunt Jenn, handing a pug to each man. The men cradled the tiny dogs to their chests.

"As you know, your pugs don't need their hair trimmed," said Aunt Jenn. "But I did bathe them and wash their face folds. I cleaned their ears and clipped their whiskers and nails."

"Thanks very much," said the bald biker.

"Ditto," said the biker with the mustache.

"We're all paid up, right, brother?" the bald biker asked Tony. Tony gave a wave and a nod.

The men put on their motorcycle helmets.

Then they pulled out two
little pairs of goggles
from their jacket pockets
and put one on each pug.
Zack and Zeke wagged
their curly tails happily.

"Okay, Ms. J. We're out of
here," the bald biker said.

"We're ready to ride!" the other said.

The girls and everyone else in the waiting
room watched as the bikers went out to the
street, strapped the pugs into a carrier on the
back of one of the motorcycles and drove off.

"And now, my favorite girls," said Aunt Jenn,
with a big smile, "please step into my office for
a moment."

The room had two large grooming tables and
two stand dryers. There were tables holding
baskets of clippers, shavers, grooming brushes,
shampoo bottles and other equipment.

"Thanks for coming, Kitty-Kat," said Aunt Jenn, using her special name for Kat. "And you, Maya and Grace. It is so nice to be able to count on my terrific trio!"

"We're always happy to help," said Kat, with a grin. "And we're excited to find out what you want us to do."

"Well, like always, I need help with a puppy who has come to stay," said Aunt Jenn. "Tony is wonderful. He's helping out a lot with phone calls, bookings and collecting payment. He can pop in to check on the puppy in the mornings, before the day gets too crazy. And in the evening I can bring the puppy and its kennel upstairs to my apartment and look after him at night."

Aunt Jenn spread out her hands. "But as you girls know, that's not quite enough. That's why I need your help once again." She popped a piece of bubble gum in her mouth. "This time we have a Yorkshire terrier puppy staying with us until

14

Saturday evening. Cricket is three months old. All Yorkies are small, even when they are full-grown. And Yorkie puppies can be tiny. Cricket doesn't even weigh as much as a block of butter."

"Oh," cooed Maya.

"But don't underestimate him," said Aunt Jenn. "He has lots of energy. More than ten packages of jumping beans!" The girls giggled. "So what do you think? Would you be able to play with Cricket and take him to the park?"

Aunt Jenn blew a pink bubble with her gum.

"Yes!" said Kat excitedly. "We'd love to."

Maya and Grace nodded enthusiastically.

"So come along, and I'll introduce you," said Aunt Jenn.

Quickly she opened the door and strode back through the waiting room, her ponytail bobbing. She led the girls down the hall and into the doggy-daycare room. It was large, with windows that looked out on a big backyard. The room had a large fenced-in area, like a playpen. A stairway led up to Aunt Jenn's apartment and a big room for puppy training.

Four large kennels lined one wall of the room. In one of the kennels was a little plush dog bed.

Kat couldn't even see the puppy until they moved closer. There, curled up in one corner of the bed, was a tiny black and tan Yorkie.

"Oh, my," whispered Grace. "Is that Cricket? He's sound asleep!"

The girls and Aunt Jenn stood looking down at the bundle of puppy.

"He really is tiny," said Maya softly.

Just then, Cricket began to stir. He yawned, but didn't open his eyes. Lying on his side, he stretched. He stuck out both of his front legs. Then he did the same with his back legs.

Cricket yawned again. He opened his eyes.

"Hello there, you," said Kat.

At once, Cricket sprang up and wagged his tail. His ears perked up. His black eyes shone.

Kat laughed. She clasped her hands together. Cricket was so sweet with his dark little button eyes and his black button nose.

Aunt Jenn reached in and picked up the puppy. "So, here he is!" She stroked Cricket's head. "Cricket's owner, Shelley, is studying to be a dentist. She has been here in Orchard Valley for a few weeks doing a short work placement with Dr. Cory. Dr. Cory is sending Shelley to a three-day conference out of town, but Shelley doesn't have any friends or family here. So she asked me to board Cricket from today, Thursday, until Saturday evening."

Aunt Jenn looked into Cricket's eyes. "What do you think, pup? Would you like these girls to play with you and take you for walks?"

Cricket squirmed excitedly. Kat saw a little pink tongue dart out and kiss Aunt Jenn's cheek.

"Okey-dokey, then," said Aunt Jenn. "If you girls are sure you can handle this big, fierce, unfriendly creature . . ."

"I think we can manage," Kat laughed.

"Well, Cricket's leash is hanging there, and the dog treats are over there, as usual," Aunt Jenn said, pointing. "Now, here is little Cricket. And off I must go!"

Aunt Jenn handed Cricket to Kat. Blowing another pink bubble with her gum, Aunt Jenn gave a wave and rushed back to her clients.

# CHAPTER THREE

"He weighs nothing!" Kat exclaimed. "I feel like I'm holding a little bird!"

Grace hurried over. She gently stroked the puppy with the tips of her fingers. "Oh, he's so tiny! And so soft!"

Maya held her hand alongside Cricket. "He's not much longer than my whole hand," she said.

Cricket loved all the attention. He sat quietly in Kat's arms as the girls patted him. He almost looked like he was outlined in black. His back and neck, and the top of his head and between his eyes, were black. The rest of him was a beautiful warm brown.

In a moment, Cricket began to squirm.

"Okay. Down you go," said Kat.

When Cricket's feet touched the floor, he raced over to investigate the shelves. Suddenly he noticed his leash on the first shelf. Curious, he poked his nose at it. The leash fell to the floor. Cricket backed away at once, his paws scrabbling on the floor. He yipped, once, twice, without taking his eyes off it.

Then, slowly, bravely, he approached the leash, yipping again.

"He's very feisty," said Maya, impressed.

Kat nodded. "That's common with Yorkshire terriers. Actually, the breed comes from an area called Yorkshire, which is in northern England. There used to be a lot of coal mines there and

Yorkshire terriers were really good at chasing rats out of the mines and mills. Even though the Yorkies were small, they would stand up to the fiercest, biggest rats."

Maya grinned at Kat. "Thank you, *Dog Breeds of the World*."

That was Kat's favorite book of all time. She had probably read *Dog Breeds of the World* at least one hundred times, and she also spent hours reading about dogs on the Internet. She was trying to learn as much about dogs as she could.

Grace shivered. "Ugh. Rats."

Cricket yipped again at the leash. Then he dashed toward it, pounced and grabbed it between his teeth. He began to shake it from side to side.

"Hey, you brave puppy!" cried Kat. "You got it! You got that nasty old leash. But now you have to let go or you'll ruin it." She crouched down beside Cricket and tried to pry the leash away. It was impossible.

22

"Here, Cricket!" called Maya. She patted her knees. She jumped up and down. She shuffled her feet. "Come here! Come and get me!" Maya took a few quick steps away from Cricket.

Cricket's eyes lit up. The Yorkie pup dropped the leash and skittered after Maya. Maya pranced across the room and back, with Cricket enjoying the chase.

"Good one, Maya!" cried Grace, scooping up the leash.

"Hey, let's take Cricket to the park right now," suggested Kat. "It's still early, and he has lots of energy."

"Okay," agreed Maya. "My mom isn't expecting me home until later. I told her I was coming here. She knew I was hoping that your aunt would ask us to help out with a puppy today."

"Same with me," said Grace.

"Great," said Kat. "How about you put the

leash on Cricket, and off we go!"

After telling Tony where they were taking the puppy, the girls headed to the park. Tails Up was on the main street of Orchard Valley. The park was a bit of a walk from there. Kat's house was only a few blocks from the park. Maya lived on the other side of town, past the school. They weren't neighbors. But that didn't stop them from spending a lot of time together.

Grace's house was on one of the streets that ran beside the park. When Grace became friends with Kat and Maya, Grace had told her new friends that her family moved to town to be closer to her grandparents. She said that living beside a park was the next best thing to living on a farm.

The distance to the park wasn't far, but the walk took some time. Cricket saw a leaf whirling past and he pounced on it. Then he saw another. He ran to the other side of Grace to get that one, too. Then there was another and another. Cricket ran between Grace's legs and around again. In a moment, Grace and Cricket were tangled up in the leash.

Kat helped Grace unwind the leash and they walked on for a few moments. Then Cricket scooted straight into a hedge. He vanished among the low branches and leaves.

"One Cricket, missing in action!" Maya laughed.

"Come on, Cricket," called Grace. "Here, little guy!" she pulled gently on the leash.

Cricket came bounding out, proudly holding an apple core in his mouth.

"Oh no!" cried Kat. She bent down and tried to take the apple core from Cricket. The more she tried to pry it from his mouth, the harder he gripped. "You are very stubborn for such a tiny puppy," she told him.

"Try making a trade," suggested Maya. "It's the only thing that seems to work."

Kat pulled a dog treat out of her pocket. "Oh, look what I have, Cricket!" she said, enticingly. "A treat for you!" She held the treat near the puppy. Immediately he dropped the apple core and delicately took the treat from Kat's palm. "Well done," she praised him.

"Okay, now off we go!" Grace cried. And off they headed again.

This time they walked about a block before Cricket suddenly lay down on the sidewalk. He put his chin down on his paws. He looked up at the girls, and his beautiful brown eyes said, "I am tired."

"You sweet thing," said Maya. "I'll carry you for a while, okay?" She picked up the puppy and exclaimed, "Oh, your hair is like silk, and you're as light as a feather! Cricket, you could slip into my backpack before school, and I'd never even know you were there."

In just a few more minutes, the girls reached the park.

"Now, down you go," said Maya, setting Cricket on the grass. "I hope that rest was just enough."

Cricket's eyes sparkled. His ears tilted this way and that. He was almost shivering with excitement.

"Time to run!" Kat cried. "Okay? Ready?"

"Ready!" Maya replied. "One, two, three . . ."

"Go!" cried Grace, and off the three girls ran, with Cricket racing alongside them.

# CHAPTER FOUR

The girls played with Cricket for the rest of the afternoon. They let him chase the blowing leaves. They threw sticks for him. Cricket was full of energy. Kat laughed seeing his little legs race so quickly here and there. He was so tiny and yet so full of life.

After a while, they took the Yorkie pup to Kat's favorite spot — the grove on the top of the hill.

"Oh, good," said Grace, yawning. "Let's sit down for a minute."

The girls got comfortable. They gazed out over the houses at the fields in the distance. *It's always so relaxing up here,* Kat thought, with a happy sigh.

A little breeze stirred the leaves on the trees. Several orange and yellow leaves twirled and fell to the ground.

Kat giggled as Cricket pounced on them, one after another. "You're like a little kitten," she teased the puppy.

"A fierce kitten," Maya corrected, smiling.

Then suddenly Cricket curled up and went to sleep.

"Oh, lucky puppy." Grace yawned. "I wish I could fall asleep as easily as that."

"What do you mean?" Kat asked.

"Oh, nothing," Grace said quickly.

"You have trouble sleeping?" Maya asked.

Grace got up and began gathering some of the colorful leaves. "No, forget it. It's nothing."

Maya frowned and crossed her arms. She was about to say something else to Grace.

*Oh no,* thought Kat. *Here we go again.* Maya and Grace were . . . well, they didn't completely get along.

"Hey, I've just remembered a joke," Kat blurted out.

Grace looked relieved. "Oh no," she groaned playfully.

"Yeah, here goes: What did the tree say to the

playful puppy?" asked Kat.

"Okay. Tell us. We know it's going to be bad," said Maya. "We're ready."

"Leaf me alone!" cried Kat.

"Ack!" choked Grace.

"So bad," agreed Maya.

The girls began chatting happily about their favorite dog breeds. A little while later, Cricket woke up.

"Cricket!" cried Maya. "Hello again!" The puppy wagged his tail and jumped into Maya's lap. Maya squealed and patted his little head. She picked him up and kissed him. "Oh, my goodness. You are so cute!"

The three girls and the puppy ran back down the hill. They played together for a while longer.

"I can't believe how much energy Cricket has!" said Kat.

The Yorkie grabbed a stick that was about four times as long as him. He could only lift one

end of it because it was
so heavy and long. But that didn't stop him
from playing with it. He did his best to drag it
across the grass.

"Come on, Cricket," Grace told him. "That's a
giant stick for a tiny puppy."

"Yes. Just leave it," said Maya. "It's too big for
you!"

Cricket refused to give up. Kat looked around.
There was nothing to trade for the stick. Then
she had an idea.

"One, two, . . ." she counted down. On "three,"
she and Grace called to Cricket and began to
run across the field.

Maya jogged on the spot, holding the leash.
"Come on, Cricket!" she cried. "Let's go! Let's go
and catch them!"

In a flash, Cricket dropped the stick and lifted his head. His ears perked up, and he bounded after Grace and Kat. Maya laughed and ran behind, holding the leash.

Soon it was time to head back to Tails Up. They were only halfway there when Cricket suddenly stopped again. He lay down on the sidewalk with his chin on his paws. He wagged his tail, but he didn't move.

"Tired out again?" asked Kat. "No wonder!" She scooped up Cricket. She was pleased for an excuse to carry the Yorkie pup. She lifted him close to her face and pressed her cheek against his soft fur. "You sweet thing," she murmured. She felt Cricket give her a quick kiss. He

nestled into her arms as they walked to Tails Up.

The girls said goodbye to Cricket as they set him gently in his kennel. "You'll have fun with Aunt Jenn tonight," Kat told the puppy. "And we'll be back to play with you again tomorrow afternoon."

Maya, Grace and Kat grabbed their backpacks. When they left Tails Up, Maya said goodbye. She headed down the main street toward her house.

Kat and Grace walked in the direction of the park together. Soon they reached the spot where Grace turned left toward her house. "See you tomorrow at school, Kat," said Grace.

Suddenly Kat had a good idea. "Hey!" she said. "I'll ask if you and Maya can come for dinner tomorrow. Then the three of us can work on the Puppy Collection after we play with Cricket. It'll be fun."

Maya and Kat had started the Puppy Collection together a short time ago. Neither girl was allowed to have a dog, but that didn't stop them from thinking about dogs all the time. They drew pictures of different breeds of puppies and downloaded photos of cute puppies from the Internet. They wrote a description of each one. They put these in a special scrapbook. When they began helping out at Tails Up, they added the puppies they met there. Grace was now their friend, so they invited her to help with the Puppy Collection, too.

"That's a great idea," said Grace. "Call me later and let me know."

"Okay," said Kat, waving goodbye.

# CHAPTER FIVE

"Have a good weekend, class," said Ms. Mitchell after the school bell rang.

"Thank you, Ms. Mitchell." "You too, Ms. Mitchell!" sang out several students.

Kat and Grace also called goodbye to their teacher before heading out of the classroom.

"Oh, I can't wait to see little Cricket," said Grace.

"Me too," Kat said.

"And thanks for asking me over for dinner and to work on the Puppy Collection," said Grace.

"It'll be fun," Kat said, grinning.

Grace put her hand over her mouth, covering a yawn.

"You're still tired," said Kat, concerned.

Grace didn't say anything. She didn't look at Kat.

The girls grabbed their backpacks and jackets. Now they stepped outside onto the playground. Kat saw Maya waiting for them at the fence, waving.

"You had trouble sleeping again last night?" Kat asked.

Grace nodded. She frowned and looked a little uncomfortable.

Just then someone tapped Kat on the arm, saying, "Hey, Kat!" Grace looked relieved that they were interrupted, like she didn't want to talk about what was bothering her.

It was Owen. He gave a funny little wave, even though he was standing right next to her. "I just wanted to say bye. And have a good weekend," he said. "And, well, see you on Monday."

Kat nodded. "Okay. Sure, Owen."

"And you too, Grace," Owen added.

"Thanks," said Grace. "You too."

"And, well, I guess that's it," said Owen.

Kat felt a little awkward. Some of the girls in her class teased her about Owen. They said he liked her. Often Owen got tongue-tied around Kat. He sometimes blushed. He reminded Maya and Kat of a basset hound, mainly because of his hat with the earflaps. He wore it all the time. Maya told Kat that Owen had lovey-dovey eyes. Especially when he looked at Kat.

*No way,* thought Kat. Owen liked her, and she liked him, too. They were friends. Nothing more.

Kat nodded again. "Okay. Thanks, Owen."

The boy stood there grinning at her. He wasn't moving. His eyes were moving from her to Grace and then back to her again. It was almost as if he wanted to say something else but didn't want to say it in front of Grace.

Kat was glad that Grace was there with her. For some reason she didn't want to know what Owen had to say.

"Okay, well . . . bye," said Kat again. She shot a look at Grace, who didn't look uncomfortable at all now. She just looked like she was trying not to giggle.

Sunjit called out from the other side of the playground, "*O-wen*. Come on, O!" He had a baseball glove in one hand and was tossing a baseball in the other.

"I have to go," Owen said apologetically. But he still didn't move.

"Right. Same with us," said Grace firmly. She grabbed Kat by the arm. "Kat and Maya and I are going to Kat's aunt's place to play with a puppy. Maya is waiting for us over there," she told Owen, pointing. Maya was standing with her hands on her hips, looking impatient.

Owen stood there, not moving, still nodding, while Grace and Kat hurried away.

Grace's giggling finally began to subside as they reached Maya.

Maya didn't even ask what was so funny. Instead she nodded knowingly at Grace and said, "Lovey-dovey eyes, right?" and Grace burst into giggles again.

Even though the joke was on her, Kat couldn't help being pleased that her two friends were sharing a joke. She pretended to frown. "Come on, you two," Kat said. "We don't want to be late at Tails Up, do we?"

The girls raced to the grooming salon, threw down their backpacks in the doggy-daycare room and hurried over to greet Cricket. He jumped to his feet and wagged his little tail happily when he saw them.

Kat lifted him from the kennel and hugged him. "Sweet, sweet puppy," she murmured. "How are you?"

She set him down, and he ran to greet Maya and then Grace. Then he tore over to the backpacks and pounced on one of the straps. He growled and flipped the strap from side to side, fiercely.

Grace laughed and rushed over. "Hey! You'll tear that! Cut that out!"

Of course the determined Yorkie wouldn't listen.

"Grace," Maya began.

"Right, right," Grace interrupted. "I know. Trade something."

She hurried to the bin of dog toys and found a squeaky toy. She squeezed it several times near the puppy and called to him in an excited voice. "Oh, look, Cricket! Look at what I have here!"

Suddenly she dropped it right beside Cricket. He couldn't resist. He dropped the strap and grabbed the squeaky toy.

"Yay!" cheered Maya.

"Good one, Grace," agreed Kat. "Now, Cricket, let's get your leash on and head to the park!"

It was a beautiful, sunny fall day, and the three girls had another fun afternoon at the park with the Yorkie puppy. He had practically bounced

all the way there. It was almost like he knew where they were going. Just like before, when they reached the park, Cricket's eyes sparkled. His ears tilted this way and that.

The girls ran across the field with him.

"I think Cricket's owner chose the perfect name for this puppy," cried Maya, who was holding his leash. "When he runs, he takes little leaps, just like a cricket!"

It had rained earlier in the afternoon. The grass was still wet. It wasn't tall, but even still, the puppy was so tiny that the grass came up to his shoulders. Soon Cricket was damp all over. His hair was already curly when it was dry. Now wet, it got even curlier.

"Oh, isn't he just the sweetest thing?" said Kat, grinning.

The girls threw a stick for the puppy. Then they collected more sticks and laid them down in a row. They ran with the puppy and he jumped over the sticks, one by one.

A woman came walking through the park with her Great Dane. When Cricket saw the big dog, he barked fiercely. He stood his ground when the Dane looked curiously at him.

"Yip, yip!" Cricket warned.

The woman smiled. "You win, little guy!" she called, leading her giant dog away. "You're too ferocious for my Brutus!"

The girls laughed.

Soon it was time to head back to Tails Up. Like the day before, Cricket didn't have the energy to walk more than a few blocks. This time it was Grace who picked him up.

"You're wet and dirty, but I don't mind," she told the puppy, planting a kiss on the top of his head.

Kat smiled, watching her friend melting with love for the tired, scruffy puppy.

# CHAPTER SIX

"I don't think I should set Cricket down," said Grace, as they entered Tails Up. She was still carrying the Yorkie pup. "He's too mucky. He'll make the floor dirty."

"I agree," said Tony, standing behind the reception counter. "That puppy needs a bath. And pronto!"

Two customers were waiting with their dogs in the lobby. They nodded their heads in agreement.

"And if we do it, it will save Aunt Jenn the trouble," said Kat. She was excited. She had never given a puppy a bath before.

"Let me see. Your aunt is using the grooming room," said Tony thoughtfully. "She's giving a standard poodle a new hairstyle. And there isn't a sink in the doggy-daycare room." Suddenly his face brightened. "I know! Cricket is so tiny, you could probably give him a wash in the bathroom sink."

"Good idea," said Kat, pleased.

Marmalade was relaxing on the counter, sneering disdainfully at the filthy puppy. "Oh, you'd like a bath too, Marmalade?" said Tony, with a wink at the girls. "When Cricket is all cleaned up, it might be your turn for a wash."

The tabby cat rose, put her tail up in the air, stalked to the other end of the counter, and then lay down again in a huff.

The girls laughed. "I thought that's what she'd

say," Tony said, grinning. He handed Kat a bottle from under the counter. "Dog shampoo. And you can grab some towels from the shelf there," he said, pointing.

Kat, Maya and Grace crowded into the bathroom with Cricket. Maya filled the sink with lukewarm water. Grace held the shampoo.

"Okay, little guy. In you go," said Kat. Gently but firmly she placed Cricket into the sink. The little puppy shivered nervously as he stood in the water, but he looked up at her trustingly. "Oh, good boy," she praised him.

Grace poured a few drops of shampoo on the Yorkie's wet back. Maya rubbed it in, working especially on his back and legs.

"Be careful not to get any water in his eyes or ears," said Kat.

"Yes, let's keep away from his head altogether," agreed Grace.

"Oh, hey!" cried Maya. "I almost forgot! I

brought my camera along this afternoon!"

She ran out of the room but was back almost right away, camera in hand. "I want to take some pictures for the Puppy Collection," she explained.

She snapped away as Grace and Kat continued to wash Cricket.

"He looks so tiny when he's wet," murmured Grace. "Tinier than tiny!"

"Yes," agreed Kat. "There's not much to him under all that fur."

Maya took a few more photos, and then she

said, "Are you almost finished? We don't want the little guy to get cold."

"Done!" exclaimed Kat. "The bath water is muddy, and you're clean as clean can be," she told Cricket.

Kat held the towel open. Grace scooped up Cricket and placed him in Kat's arms. Kat wrapped the towel around the pup and began drying him.

"Oh, look at his head poking out," said Grace. "Cricket, you are adorable."

Soon Cricket was back in his kennel, dry, curled up and napping.

When the girls said goodbye to Tony, he told them he'd see them tomorrow. "And you can count on Marmalade being here, too," he joked.

Kat, Maya and Grace chatted all the way to Kat's house.

"Half an hour until dinner!" Kat's mother said, after greeting Kat and her friends.

"That means we have a little time to do some work on the Puppy Collection right now," suggested Kat, as she and the girls ran upstairs to her bedroom.

"Let's look at the Tails Up puppies that we've helped with, first," suggested Maya. The girls flipped through the pages of the scrapbook.

They looked at pictures they had drawn of Bailey, the Labrador retriever pup, and Riley, the golden retriever puppy. They read their descriptions of the sheltie pup, Murphy, and the three bichon frise puppies, Chantal, Aimée and Bijou. They looked at the photos of the Bernese mountain dog, Piper, in the puppy event of the local dog show.

"Oh, all these puppies were so sweet," sighed Kat.

"Let's work on creating pages for Cricket," suggested Grace. "What about the description? How about something like this: 'Cricket is a

Yorkshire terrier puppy. He is three months old. He is mostly tan and black, with a black button nose and brown button eyes. He is tiny but he stands up for himself. He's . . .'" Grace paused. "What's the right word here?"

"Feisty!" said Kat. "And self-confident."

"Yes!" Maya jumped up and threw her hands

out wide. "He has self-confidence to the max."

Kat and Grace laughed. "Like when Cricket barked at the Great Dane?" Kat asked.

*"Exactamente,"* said Maya.

Soon, Kat's father called upstairs for the girls to come down for dinner. They all enjoyed a nice meal. Then Kat's mother took Aidan, Kat's older brother, to his basketball game. The girls went back upstairs and did some more work on the Puppy Collection.

But it wasn't much longer until Kat noticed Grace rubbing her eyes. Then Grace said, "I'm going to head home now, Kat. Thanks again for dinner."

Maya frowned. "Really? Why so early?"

Grace didn't say anything for a minute. Then she said, "I'm just really tired."

"But why?" Maya insisted.

Grace reached down for her backpack. She didn't look at Maya.

"Maya," said Kat. "She doesn't have to say." Maya frowned. "Although I wish you would tell us, Grace," Kat added. "Maybe we could help. It might help to talk about it."

"Is it something about us? Something we did or said? Something I did?" Maya asked.

Grace stood up. Her arms were straight down. Her hands were in fists. She shook her head. "Bye, Kat," Grace said. "Bye, Maya. See you both tomorrow."

Kat recognized the signs. She used to think this meant Grace was angry. Now she knew it was the way Grace looked when she was upset or embarrassed.

"Okay, Grace," said Kat hastily. She jumped up. "Good. So you're still coming to Tails Up in the morning to play with Cricket?"

"Yes," Grace said slowly. She hesitated. Still, she didn't look up. "Unless you don't want me to."

"No! No!" Kat stammered. "We do. I mean,

no, it's not that we don't want you to. Of course we want you to come."

"Okay," said Grace. "Thanks for dinner. And bye."

Grace left the room. Kat hurried after her to see her out. When she came back, Maya was grumpy.

"What's up with her anyway?" Maya asked.

Kat shook her head. "I don't know," she said.

"How come she won't tell us if something is wrong?" asked Maya. "Aren't we her friends?"

Kat sighed and lifted her shoulders. "I don't know," she repeated. "I hope so."

# CHAPTER SEVEN

When Kat arrived at Tails Up on Saturday morning, Tony was busy on the phone. But when he pointed at the doggy-daycare room and held up two fingers, Kat knew that Maya and Grace must have already arrived. She smiled at the receptionist, stroked grumpy Marmalade's head and hurried to meet her friends.

Grace was holding Cricket, who was squirming with excitement. Maya was trying to clip the

Yorkie pup's leash to his collar.

"Look at his tail. It's wagging faster than is actually humanly possible," said Maya. "I mean, doggily possible."

Grace giggled.

Kat grinned and breathed a sigh of relief. She had been worried about how they would all get along this morning. But both her friends looked happy. Maybe everything was okay with Grace now.

They made a plan. Spend some time at Tails Up, then go to the park. Come back for lunch. Then go back to the park.

They rolled balls for Cricket in the doggy-daycare room. They set up an obstacle course

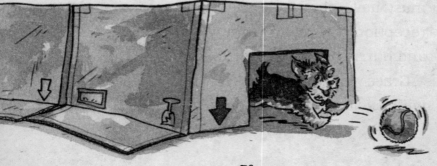

with chairs. The puppy weaved in and out of them, following the girls. They made a tunnel with boxes, and he chased a ball through it.

Next, they headed to the park. They all ran across the field three times. The girls thought Cricket must be getting tired. However, when a little girl dropped her snack bag of crackers, the wind blew it toward them — and Cricket pounced. He shook the bag back and forth, crackers flying. He seemed to love the crinkly sound it made.

By the time the girls got the bag away from the puppy, the crackers were gone. Kat apologized to the little girl and her mother. But the little girl didn't cry. She was clapping her hands, cheering, "Doggy! Doggy!"

Ready for a rest, the girls headed up the hill with Cricket. When they reached the top, they sat and looked out over the countryside. Kat put Cricket on her tummy, and he instantly fell asleep. Maya took one photo, and then another, for the Puppy Collection.

When they ran back down the hill again, it was Kat's turn to take photos.

They all realized they were hungry at the same time. As they headed back to Tails Up, the girls talked about puppies and tried to decide what kind of dog they would get one day.

Grace began to talk about her farm dog, Bella. She had died that spring, before Grace moved to Orchard Valley. "Bella was a mix of several breeds. She was just perfect for me. I still can't imagine having any other dog than her," admitted Grace.

"Well, I think I'd like a King Charles spaniel," said Maya. "Or maybe a Yorkie, like sweet little Cricket. Or, no. Maybe a plain old hound dog. One that throws its head back and howls. Ah-ooooo!" Maya demonstrated, her chin high, her eyes closed.

Cricket froze in his tracks. He stared up at Maya in alarm.

Ooo Ooooo...

Kat and Grace burst out laughing.

"Come on, little guy," Kat said, gently. "She's nothing to be afraid of. Well, most of the time!"

The girls said hello to Tony as they headed into the doggy-daycare room.

"I'm exhausted," said Maya. "How can one tiny, little puppy have so much energy!"

"Good question," said Grace. She unclipped Cricket's leash. The puppy raced over to his water bowl and began to drink.

"Hey, did you know that dogs don't actually scoop water up and into their mouths with their tongues when they drink?" asked Kat. She watched Cricket's little tongue lap at the water. "It looks like that. But they're really curling their tongues the other way. A dog puts its tongue into the water and then lifts it  up really fast. A stream of water attaches to its tongue and rises, but only for less than a second. The water starts to drop back down into the bowl. The dog has to snap its mouth shut to catch the water!"

"Thank you, Einstein," said Maya, "and *Dog Breeds of the World*!"

"That's really cool," said Grace, impressed. She stared hard, watching Cricket drink.

"You can't really see it happen live," Kat told her. "No matter how closely you look. I saw a slow motion video of it on our family computer. You both should look it up some time. It's amazing."

"That does sound amazing, Kat, but all I can think about at this moment is food," said Maya, dramatically. "Food. I need food. We all packed a lunch, yes? I'm going to run and wash my hands, and then, if I am still alive, I'll stagger back and eat. Kat-nip? Grace? Coming?" she called behind her as she left.

"Sure," said Kat. "I'll just put Cricket back in the kennel first."

"Oh, it's okay," said Grace. "I'll stay with Cricket while you go and wash up with Maya. Then you can both stay with Cricket while I go."

"Okay," said Kat. She and Maya went and

washed their hands. As they were heading back to the doggy-daycare room, Tony called to them. He explained that he was busy booking a grooming appointment for a client. He asked if they could help another client carry bags of dog food to her car.

"Sure," said Kat.

"Your wish is our command," said Maya, with a grin.

After helping with the bags, Maya and Kat returned to the doggy-daycare room. Grace was speaking on a cellphone. "Okay, Mom. See you soon," she said. She dropped the cellphone into her backpack and threw her bag over her shoulder.

"What's up?" asked Kat.

"You have a cellphone?" Maya asked, surprised.

"It's my mom's phone. She's letting me borrow it for a while," Grace said. "And guess what? I have to go." Her voice sounded strange.

Maya just looked at Grace. She didn't say anything.

"You have to go right now?" Kat asked, puzzled. "Why?"

"Well . . . I forgot that we're going to my grandmother's for lunch today," Grace said. "My mom wants me to come. Then she'll bring me back again."

Kat frowned. She wasn't sure she believed her friend.

Maya made a face. "Really?" she asked. "You really forgot?"

"I'll be back soon. But I have to go right now. My mom's coming to get me. She's going to pull up out front," said Grace.

"Okay, sure," Kat said.

And then Grace was gone.

# CHAPTER EIGHT

"What's up with Grace? That was weird," said Maya. "But, oh, well. I'm starving, and I'm going to eat." She opened her backpack, pulled out her lunch bag and began to enjoy her sandwich.

Kat sat down on the floor beside her and began to munch on her carrot sticks. Cricket was curled up in a ball near his kennel, sleeping.

"Don't you just love watching him sleep?

asked Maya. "You can see his sides go in and out when he breathes."

Kat nodded. The puppy twitched. "He must be dreaming about playing at the park with us," she said.

Kat was happy Maya didn't want to talk about Grace. She didn't either. She was afraid to tell Maya what she was thinking. That maybe Maya was right. That Grace was keeping something from them. If she said it out loud, it might make it real. It might ruin their friendship.

Cricket woke up as the girls finished eating. He gave a big yawn, stretching out his front legs. The puppy stood up and slowly stuck out one back leg and then the other. He shook himself hard, and the girls giggled. "He almost fell over!" said Maya. She went over and picked up the puppy. "Ready for some more fun?" she asked him, stroking him gently.

"Hey, you must be hungry, Cricket!" said Kat.

"Aunt Jenn said to give him a little of this puppy food." She got a bag of dog food from the shelf and poured some into Cricket's bowl.

Maya put him down, and he came bounding over and sniffed at it. But he didn't eat any food.

"Not hungry yet?" asked Maya. "Well, I guess we need to help you work up an appetite." She picked up a squeaky toy and threw it across the room. "There you go, Cricket. Go get it!"

The puppy's ears perked up. He raced after the toy and pounced on it. He held it down with his front paws and chewed on it. Then he picked

it up in his teeth and shook it from side to side.

"Okay, now this one," said Kat, squeaking a plastic ball.

Cricket froze and listened carefully, cocking his head to one side.

Kat squeaked the ball again.

Cricket dropped his toy and came bounding over to Kat. Kat showed Cricket the ball, squeaked it again and tossed it to the other side of the room. The puppy bounded after it.

The girls took turns throwing toys for the puppy. Then they played hide-and-seek with Cricket. They hid a toy and helped Cricket search for it. They snapped on his leash and practiced walking nicely with him.

When Cricket curled up for another nap, Kat went to her backpack and pulled out a bottle of juice. "Grace should be back soon," she said. "Do you want to take Cricket to the park when she gets here?"

Maya didn't answer. She was looking worried. She was searching all the pockets on the outside of her backpack. Then she began digging inside it.

"What's wrong?" asked Kat.

Maya turned her backpack upside down and shook it. Out dropped a notepad, several gel pens, four shiny rocks, some coins and a sparkly hair band.

"What is it?" asked Kat.

"It's gone." Maya stood up. She crossed her arms. "I can't believe she took it. It's gone."

"What's gone? Who took it?" Kat asked.

"Grace. There was a chocolate bar here, in the pocket of my backpack, and now it's gone," Maya growled.

"Hey," said Kat uneasily, "why would you think Grace took it? You don't know she took it."

"Where else would it have gone? Did you take it, Kat-nip?" Maya asked, fiercely.

"No, of course not," Kat said.

"Okay, then where else would it go?" Maya demanded.

Just then, Cricket whimpered. He was crying out in his sleep.

Suddenly, Kat had a terrible thought. *Oh no. Oh no. Could Cricket have eaten the chocolate bar?*

"Where was your backpack? And where was

the chocolate bar?" Kat asked quickly, jumping to her feet.

"The chocolate bar was in the side pocket of my backpack. And my backpack was just sitting here on the floor. Beside yours," Maya said. "Why?"

"So Cricket could have reached it? Cricket could have grabbed the chocolate bar?" Kat asked, slowly.

"Yes, I guess so," Maya said. "But where would the wrapper be now?"

"Puppies eat anything," said Kat. "Cricket might have eaten it." Her voice trembled. "It's just the kind of thing he'd do. He loves grabbing things. He'd probably love the crinkly sound of the chocolate bar wrapper."

"But when would he have got it? We've been with him almost constantly," Maya said.

"Well, maybe this morning before we went to the park. We all went in and out of here a few times — to talk to Aunt Jenn, to use the bathroom." Kat wrapped her arms around her stomach. She felt sick. "And before lunch. You and I went to wash our hands and then we helped load those dog food bags into the client's car. Grace was here, but she was on the phone with her mom for a bit. Maybe she wasn't paying attention to Cricket."

"Okay," said Maya. "So let's say he did eat the chocolate bar. So what? What's the worst thing that could happen?"

Kat swallowed. She took a deep breath. "Chocolate can be poisonous to dogs."

The color drained from Maya's face. "Oh," she said. "Oh no." She hurried over to Cricket. Kat followed. "But the little guy looks okay," Maya said. "He's sleeping. Would one chocolate bar really hurt him?"

"Chocolate has a chemical in it called theobromine," Kat explained. "Also caffeine, like in coffee. Those two things can be really toxic for dogs. The more the dog eats, the more it's affected. The smaller the dog, the more it's affected. The type of chocolate also makes a difference."

"It was milk chocolate," said Maya.

"That's good. It's the least toxic," said Kat. "But Cricket is so small that even one bar of milk chocolate could harm him."

Maya crouched beside the puppy. "How would we know if he had chocolate poisoning?" she asked Kat.

Kat tried to remember. "He might throw up. He might have diarrhea or pee a lot. He might have an upset stomach or drool. He might be nervous or restless."

"He hasn't done any of those things. And he's even sleeping now. That's a good sign," said Maya.

"Yes, but I'm not an expert," Kat said. "I don't

know how long it would take the chocolate to affect him. It could be that he ate the bar but just hasn't started having symptoms yet." Her voice shook. "And he didn't eat any of his own dog food, did he? Maybe he was too full of chocolate or the chocolate bar upset his stomach. Either way, not good." She crouched down beside Cricket. "Did you eat that chocolate bar, little guy?" she asked the sleeping puppy, softly. "The bar, the wrapper, the whole thing? Did you?"

"I bet Grace took it," Maya said, firmly. "I'm sure she's been keeping secrets from us over the last few days. You think so too, right? So why not take a chocolate bar and not tell us?"

"I don't know. I don't know," said Kat. "It seems different somehow. Like stealing. I don't think Grace would do that." She was trying to stay calm, but she could feel panic setting in. "I wish we could just ask Grace."

"She'll be back soon, right?" Maya asked.

"Why don't we wait and ask her, and if she didn't take it, then we'll go straight to Aunt Jenn?"

Kat paused. "Waiting might be risky."

"But your aunt is so busy," said Maya. "And won't she be mad? It's pretty dumb of me to leave a chocolate bar in my backpack on the floor where Cricket could get it." Maya's lips began to quiver. "If we tell your aunt, she might never let us come back and help with the puppies again. And it would be all my fault!"

Maya looked so upset that Kat stepped closer to comfort her.

"Maya, it was a simple mistake," Kat said. "No one will blame you." She put her arm around her friend's shoulders.

"But what if Cricket gets really sick? What if he dies?" Maya cried.

Kat had been hoping Maya would decide what was best. But now she realized she had to take charge. And it was clear to her what they had to do.

"Maya, that's why we have to tell Aunt Jenn. Right now." Kat looked Maya in the eyes. "We have to tell her that it's possible Cricket ate a chocolate bar. We can't wait for Grace to show up. Okay?"

Maya nodded. "I know. You're right. I'm just scared." She looked over at Cricket, who was still asleep. "We have to make sure Cricket is going to be okay."

# CHAPTER NINE

"Hi, Kat! Hi, Maya! I'm back," Grace announced, bursting into the doggy-daycare room. But as soon as she saw the two girls, her face dropped. "What happened?" she asked. "What's wrong?"

Kat rushed over to Grace. "Oh, Grace, we're so happy to see you! We think Cricket may have eaten a chocolate bar from the pocket of Maya's backpack."

"Chocolate can be poisonous, especially to

little dogs like him," said Maya. "We were just about to go and tell Aunt Jenn!"

"Oh," said Grace. Her arms were straight at her sides.

Maya looked at her closely. "Did you eat the chocolate bar, Grace? You did, didn't you?"

"No," Grace said. Her face looked hard.

"I don't believe you!" Maya cried. "How can you lie about this?"

Grace put her hands on her hips. "I'm not lying! I said I didn't take it, and that's the truth. But I do know where it is! Just before my mom called earlier, Cricket was sniffing around your backpack. The little guy grabbed the chocolate bar right out of the pocket!"

Kat gasped. *Oh no. Cricket ate the chocolate. He . . . he might . . .*

Kat stared at Maya, and Maya stared back.

Grace went on. "You know how hard it is to get anything away from that puppy!" She glanced

over at him. He was still sleeping soundly. "I had to grab a squeaky toy from the bin and squeeze it a million times, and throw it in the air and drop it. He finally dropped the chocolate bar and grabbed the squeaky toy instead. And I put the chocolate bar up high, where I knew he couldn't get at it!" Grace pointed to the top shelf of the wall unit. "Then Mom called, and I had to leave quickly. I'm so sorry I didn't tell you, but I'm not lying! I didn't steal it from you!"

"So, Cricket took the chocolate bar, really? But you got it away, and he didn't eat any of it?" Maya asked.

"Yes," Grace said, nodding.

"Oh, thank goodness!" Maya cried. She slapped her hand to her chest.

Kat breathed a sigh of relief. *He's okay. Cricket's okay.*

Then Maya looked at Grace fiercely. "Why didn't you tell us? We were so worried."

"I'm sorry I didn't tell you." Grace looked straight into Maya's eyes. "I just didn't think it would matter. I didn't know chocolate was poisonous to dogs. I didn't know you might think he'd taken it. And I had to leave in a hurry."

"That's okay, Grace," Kat said. "Everything's all right now. Maya didn't know that about chocolate either. And Cricket is all right. That's the most important thing."

But Maya was still upset. "We were scared,

Grace! We were scared that Cricket might get sick from the chocolate. And we were scared about telling Aunt Jenn that he might have eaten it while we were supposed to be looking after him!"

Grace nodded. She rubbed her eyes. She looked like she was going to cry.

Maya went on, "But I shouldn't have accused you of stealing the chocolate bar. And I should have believed you when you said you didn't." She put her hand on Grace's arm. "I'm sorry, Grace."

Grace gave a tiny smile. "That's okay."

"You actually saved Cricket's life. Didn't she, Kat?" Maya said.

"She did," Kat agreed, grinning.

"And I was wrong to be afraid of telling Aunt Jenn about Cricket." Maya shook her head again. "It was dumb. I hate having people mad at me, and I didn't want Aunt Jenn to be angry. I was afraid of getting in trouble."

"Well, I've been afraid of telling you both something, too," Grace said. "It's why I'm so tired. I was so worried about my grandmother. She's been sick, and she had to have an operation yesterday. My mom called me just before lunch and said we could go and see her . . ."

"Oh, Grace," said Kat. "Your grandmother is really sick? That's awful."

"Except she's going to be okay," Grace said. She took a deep breath. "We found out when we went to the hospital just now."

Maya nodded. "Good," she said. "That's good. That's really good."

Grace wiped away a tear.

"But why didn't you tell us before?" Kat asked. "When you were over for dinner."

"That's what I mean about being afraid," Grace explained. "I couldn't tell you about my grandmother. I wasn't afraid of what you and Maya would say. I *wanted* to tell you, but . . . the

words wouldn't come out. It was like if I didn't say it, it wouldn't be real."

Kat put her arm around Grace. "That's okay. I know just what you mean."

"I wish I had told you both, though." Grace's voice was shaky. "I think it might have made me feel better. Telling you two. Telling my friends."

Just then Cricket yawned and opened his eyes.

The tiny puppy did a big stretch, his front legs stiff, his rear end in the air.

The girls giggled. He looked so cute.

Kat picked up Cricket. "You silly thing," she scolded. "Scaring us like that, stealing that chocolate bar. It's a good thing Grace saw you and took it away from you!"

She snuggled the little Yorkie, and he wagged his tail. He licked her nose. She carried him to Grace and placed the puppy in her friend's arms. Somehow she knew that would make everything better.

And of course telling them did make Grace feel better, too. Grace buried her face in the puppy's soft fur. When she looked up again, she had a big grin on her face. Then Cricket began wiggling in Grace's arms. She set him down. The Yorkie puppy raced over to his leash. He pounced on it, grabbed it between his teeth and began to shake it from side to side.

"Well, you know what I think?" asked Maya, her arms crossed, her voice stern. She was looking at Grace.

*Oh no!* thought Kat. *What is Maya going to say?*

"I'm really glad your grandmother is going to be okay. I'm glad you told us now. And we need to take this crazy puppy back to the park right this second!" said Maya. "Look at him. He can hardly wait!"

The three girls laughed. Cricket wagged his tail happily and shook the leash from side to side again.

"Okay!" cried Kat. "Let's go!"

# CHAPTER TEN

The girls spent the rest of the afternoon playing in the park with Cricket. They took turns running back and forth across the field with the puppy. They rolled a ball for Cricket and let him chase it on his retractable leash. They took even more photos of Cricket for the Puppy Collection.

After a while, the girls flopped down under the trees at the edge of the park. Kat scooped up Cricket into her lap. The tired puppy sighed

happily and instantly fell asleep. Kat stroked his soft fur. It would be hard to say goodbye to him later today. He was such a sweet little puppy with his black button nose and dark brown eyes.

"So, Grace, when will your grandmother come home from the hospital?" asked Maya.

"Maya!" cried Kat. *Wouldn't it upset Grace to talk about this?*

But to Kat's surprise, Grace grinned. "We don't know yet, but soon. The doctor says it might only be three or four days."

"Nice," said Maya.

Kat cuddled Cricket and thought about the missing chocolate bar. Thank goodness Cricket was okay. It could have been the worst day ever. It could have been a disaster. But it wasn't. Cricket snuggled into her lap. She looked at Maya and Grace laughing together. Instead the day turned out to be a good one after all. *And, best of all*, thought Kat, giving the Yorkie a little kiss on his soft head, *it's not over yet*.